Ferguson's Tractor-biography

And Selected Ruminations

Ruminations overheard by B. T. Mole, Ph.D.
Translation from Molish by Daniel V. Runyon
Illustrations by Scott Auch

Ferguson's Tractor-biography
And Selected Ruminations
Daniel V. Runyon
Illustrations by Scott Auch

Copyright 2015 by Daniel V. Runyon

Independently published at Saltbox Press
Contact publisher at dvrunyon@gmail.com

Print ISBN: 978-1-878559-25-8
Price: $10.00 USD

Reviews

When's the last time a fictitious character "wrote" a book about herself by the hand of a Molish scribe whose pilfered text makes it into English? Fiction by imaginary characters is our version of *funny!*
—*Rye Humor*

Milking the traumas of her life, Ferguson sets forth a publication of remarkable insight and minimal froth—many good insights on which to ruminate when next you are stalled.
—*The Dairy Diary*

Who said animation is dead? Long live Ferguson!— and may tool boxes like hers be made into condominiums the world over.
—*The Rodent Register*

A harbinger of moral sensibility and religious fervor, this machine sallies forth to influence agrarian lowlife in a redemptive manner. Sensational!
—*Plantation Gazette*

The most astounding intellectual achievement in the history of farm implement scholarship, Ferguson's highly evolved cerebral prowess pushes the boundaries of wit and wisdom into the stratosphere.
—*Evolutionary Farm Implement Journal*

Dedication

To Re-weld, who has been through fire. Also for the new generation of disciples around the world who co-labor with God to fulfill the Great Commission.

Contents

Page   **Chapter**
7   Introduction

Section I: Ferguson's Tractor-biography

9   1. Lumpy Acres
17   2. Gotten Rid Of
27   3. Restored
36   4. Sold
47   5. The Cost of Discipleship
58   6. Fit for Service

Section II: Selected Ruminations

72   This World's Wisdom
77   Do Missionaries Get Mad?
81   Mileage Plus
83   Homosexual Clergy
85   How to Pick Your Dead Furrow
89   Discouraged, But Not About My Lawn
93   God Is Not Like *This* Farmer
97   A Church-Planting Recipe
101   The Yoke's On Me
104   A Cheeky Proposition
106   No-Till Theology
108   A Plot Thickens
112   A Quackgrass Church
116   Brick & Mortar vs. Hearts Of Flesh
120   Seeing Through The Steel Wool
124   One Astonished Missionary

Introduction

The Lord's hand has been upon my life, saving me from an early grave and giving me important work in my more mature years. Hence, many people have asked me to "write" my tractor-biography.

Please don't be confused by my using the third person to "write" about myself. When Dr. Mole set my ruminations into print, it came out this way. I like how this approach gives objectivity exploring a subject I am intimately familiar—myself!

I warn you, the early part of my story is sad—but that is the way of life without God. Joy creeps in along with advancing years and growing obedience.

Special thanks to Stephen and Alice Lawhead who "kicked the dirt off my fire." I am indebted to Dr. B. T. Mole for setting these words in print, as I have no fingers with which to write. And I acknowledge Daniel V. Runyon, the creator and sustainer of my universe.

Love, Ferguson

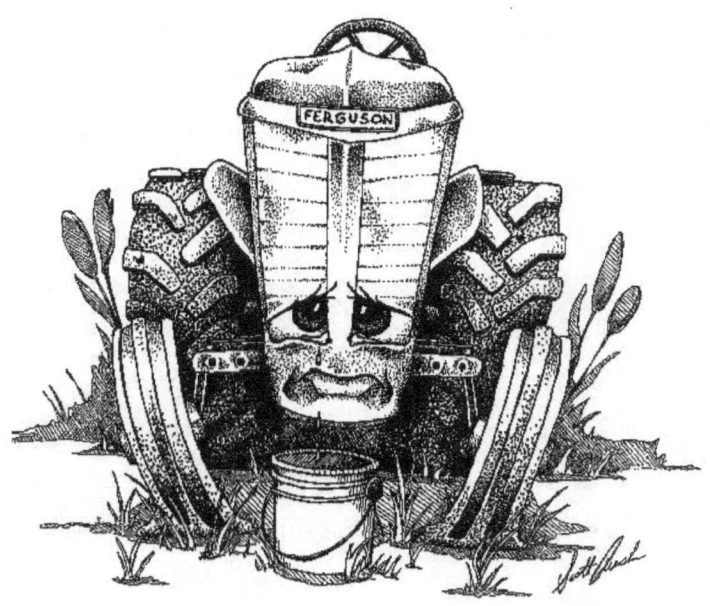

"Junk! Is that what I am?" Ferguson whimpers. She does not like the idea of being "gotten rid of." Where do you go when you are gotten rid of?

1. Lumpy Acres

Ferguson is sad, for her years at Lumpy Acres are coming to a very unpleasant and untimely end.

Once upon a time, she was a shiny new tractor. That was long ago in 1948. Now the light gray paint on her tummy is worn away from driving through fields of tall corn or wheat. Or weeds.

The smooth Ferguson-gray paint on her nose is turning dry and cracked from many years in the hot sun. Brown streaks of rust blister up in the tired lines of her skin.

Once black and firm, Ferguson's tires are now flat. They feel loose and ready to peel away from the rims. The steering wheel has frozen and thawed many times too many. Large gaps in the plastic hoop are held in place only by a thin steel core.

Her temperature gauge is broken. Tiny holes freckle her radiator. Cold snow collects on the top of her head and fenders and seat.

Poor Ferguson! No wonder she feels sad. The farmer has bought a shiny new green John Deere with a radio and air conditioned cab. He no longer cares about Ferguson. Broken down and antique, she now parks in the cold shadow of the north side of the old red workshop lean-to behind the garage.

Tall grasses and ragweed grow up between Ferguson's rear axle and under her engine block. Now dead and dry in the winter snow, the brown weeds tremble when the wind blows, and tickle her side-mounted distributor cap and brush against her spark plug wires. Poor Ferguson sneezes and sneezes, but her nose can no longer run, for it is all out of antifreeze.

In the small tool box under Ferguson's hood a sparrow builds a nest. At first it is a warm and happy feeling to have the sparrows, until the small birds grow up and fly away.

"Cheap, cheap" they rudely say, after having flown around to see the world. "Cheap, cheap. What a cheap place to live." They soon wing away, leaving Ferguson feeling empty and dirty.

* * * * *

"When are you going to get rid of that dilapidated old tractor?" the farmer's wife complains one spring day. The need to do some spring cleaning is flowing thickly in her blood. "I get tired of seeing it around! We've got to get rid of some of the junk around here...."

Ferguson overhears this frightening complaint and shivers in the shadows where she sits, rusting. "Junk. Is that what I am?" she whimpers. "What will they do to me?" The frown on her grill deepens. A tear splashes down onto the rotten threads of her front tires.

In answer to his wife, the farmer pushes back his red cap, scratches the hair above his left ear, and says, "Hummmf, hummmf."

The farmer's wife does not know what this means. Neither does Ferguson.

Several weeks pass by. The snow begins to melt, trickling into Ferguson's ears. New weeds and grass begin pushing up through the ground and into Ferguson's ruined tires. The sweet smell of sunshine warming the frosty ground rouses earthworms and awakens the crocuses. Spring is coming. Excitement and new life soak into Lumpy Acres.

Ferguson is unable to enjoy the warmth, and not just because of the cold, shaded spot where she sits. A deeper cold penetrates her damp engine block—the memory of the complaining farmer's wife who asked,

"When are you going to get rid of that dilapidated old tractor?"

Ferguson does not like the idea of being "gotten rid of." Where do you go when you are gotten rid of?

Things look very bad for Ferguson, but at least she still has all her parts. She cannot imagine how it would hurt if someone were to take away her seat, or burn her tires, or pull the gears out of her transmission.

"Oh! I am so terribly afraid," she says right out loud one dark and moonless night.

"Why are you afraid?" asks a rumbling.

Ferguson blinks her one eye that still has glass in it and looks around. There is no lightning, so she is surprised by the thunder. But it was a rumbling, not a thunder, and it comes again, very low, from the direction of the workshop. "Why are you afraid?"

"The farmer's wife wants to get rid of me," replies Ferguson, looking closely at the workshop wall for signs of life. In all this time she has not realized Workshop is alive.

"You are not so very old," says Workshop. "I remember Old Orange. He used to park just where you sit."

Ferguson looks down. So this is not the first time someone is gotten rid of. There is no sign of Old Orange now. Whatever is about to happen to Ferguson has happened before.

"Old Orange had no tires like you," Workshop continues, "just metal wheels. And no power take-off or three-point hitch either—just a belt-drive wheel. To get him started you had to turn a crank."

"Gracious me," thinks Ferguson. "What use is a tractor like that?"

She must have thought this out loud, for Workshop replies, "He was most useful indeed, in his time."

"Yes, yes!" squeals a shrill, new voice. "But his time is gone, gone, gone!" Ratter the Rat must have overheard the conversation. He scampers up Ferguson's rear tire, perches on her fender-like ears, and wails, "Old Orange is gone to pieces, pieces, pieces! I find her pieces in many places, places! Farmer welded his fender into a sled for Sonny. His steering wheel is on a soap box derby race car! His front wheels are on the old manure spreader! His seat is bolted to a stump down by the fishing pond! His flywheel is chained to the old boat for an anchor!

13

His engine oil and radiator water are bleeding into the ground beneath our very feet...."

"ENOUGH!" thunders Workshop, and a piece of wood siding swipes out at Ratter, who ducks hastily, then dives toward his hole, uninjured by Workshop's anger.

But as he scurries into the darkness, Ratter the Rat shrieks over his shoulder, "Old Orange is gone, goner, gonest! Old tractors never die—they are just gotten rid of!"

"O dear," cries Ferguson. "Oh dear me, dear me. What an awful thing it is to be gotten rid of. What an awful thing...."

Ferguson slumps on her axles, her last ounce of pride gone. No one can save her now.

2. Gotten Rid Of

"Maybe not," says thoughtful Workshop. "Maybe being gotten rid of is not such a bad thing. A tree was gotten rid of to make my boards, and rolls of steel were gotten rid of to make your fenders and hood—er, excuse me, I mean your ears and nose—."

Workshop is about to say more when the air is split by the loud crowing of Rooster Rex, and at that instant Ferguson detects the breaking of the darkness. It is not daylight yet, not by any means, but the darkest part of night is past.

"You are very kind," says Ferguson to Workshop. "That was quite a speech for you, who have sat here so long in silence."

Workshop does not reply. The effort of talking makes him very tired, so Ferguson continues, "I know that I must be gotten rid of. I suppose it must happen to all of us in the end. I will just have to make the best of it. But I truly would give anything to feel the fire in my cylinders again...."

"Don't talk to my dry boards about fire!" growls Workshop. It is not a friendly growl, and

17

Ferguson knows it is definitely the end of the conversation.

Ferguson falls asleep thinking that perhaps she is one lucky old tractor after all. Better to be gotten rid of than to live endlessly in fear of fire.

*   *   *   *   *

A car door slams, waking Ferguson from the best sleep she has enjoyed in many weeks. Then another car door slams. Farmer and his wife are getting out of the car.

"I finally went and done it," mutters Farmer as he fishes around in his shirt pocket with the first two fingers of his right hand.

"Now what have you gone an' done?" asks the wife.

"Just what you told me to," says Farmer. Instead of stomping up the side porch steps like usual, he moseys toward Workshop.

"No you never!" whines the wife. "I told you to plow the garden two weeks ago. It's time to be planting lettuce and carrots and tomatoes, but you ain't even plowed under the weeds...."

"Not that," replies Farmer, pulling a small paper from his shirt pocket. "I placed the want ad. Look," and he holds out the small paper toward his wife. Here is what she reads: "**FOR SALE:** '48 FERGUSON. SHOT. BEST OFFER."

"Humph!" she says after reading the ad. "Who would buy old Ferguson?"

"Don't know," Farmer replies. "Have to wait and see." His words linger until the air is split by the grinding of John Deere's starter and the "pop-pop-popping" of his cylinders as he and Farmer chug off to plow the garden.

Next evening around supper time the phone rings. Ferguson tunes both ears to try and hear Farmer's part of the conversation.

"Yup, 'at's my ad alright.... Oh, hi. Yes, I know of the Glick Scrap Company. Sure, recycled iron and metal and what not.... Nope, no, haven't driven her in quite a few years.... You bet, it's mor'n I want to spend fixin' 'er up.... Well, now, I can't say about that.... You want I should take $100—for scrap metal? Yeah, well, you can come on around then.... Seems kinda stingy, but we can talk...."

Farmer's wife stands with hands on hips. No sooner does Farmer hang up the phone than she quips, "Kinda stingy, nothin'! I say $100 is generous. Get rid of that eyesore while the getting's good!"

Ferguson has heard enough. She lets her ears collapse over her brittle tires. She slumps on her axles. Her last ounce of pride gone, she relaxes the gasket around her oil filter. Black, filthy engine lubricant drizzles into the earth. No one can save her now.

She sobs and sobs until her crankcase is as empty as her heart, as sorry about the selfish way she has lived as she is sad about the cruel way she is about to die.

Ratter the Rat crawls up her radiator, into the tool box under the hood, and begins making a nest for himself where the sparrows once lived. "Glick Scrap sounds like a great place to live!" Ratter announces. "I'm moving out with you, Ferguson!"

Workshop listens and shares her sorrow but says nothing.

Helpless, abused, and now in complete resignation, Ferguson turns her once good eye to the heavens, where a quarter moon gazes down upon her pitiful frame. "Maker of heaven and earth," she says, "if You really do exist, save me now and I will give You all that there is of me."

*   *   *   *   *

Come morning, a flat-bed truck pulls into the yard. The words "Glick Scrap Company" are painted in a black arch on the red door. A wiry, unshaven man in blue jeans steps out of the truck, walks up onto the porch, and knocks at the door.

"Came to pick up yer scrap," he says when Farmer steps out into the crisp morning air.

"There she is out beside the workshop," replies Farmer. "Back on around and I'll help ya load 'er up. You got the $100 payment?"

"Don't know nothin' 'bout that. I'm just a driver. George Rice. Pleased to know ya. Glick asked me to run on out here and pick up some scrap, and here I am." With that George gets back into the truck and backs across the lawn toward Ferguson.

George works in silence as he loads Ferguson. Farmer helps, positioning heavy boards for a ramp between Ferguson's front wheels and the back of the truck. Then, by means of a winch and cable, Ferguson is soon hoisted into place and ready for her ride to the Glick Scrap Company.

"Driving truck—that all you do?" Farmer asks.

"Not hardly," says George. "Mostly I'm a mechanic. Nothing easier to work on than this here Ferguson. What's wrong with it?"

"Everything's wrong, now. Needs tires, battery, everything. But it was just a leaky water pump causing trouble when I parked her out here for the last time."

George swings himself up on the truck bed and squints at the water pump. "Maybe just a bad gasket," he suggests.

"Nope," counters Farmer. "She was dripping from the impeller shaft. Probably needs a whole new water pump."

"That's only 60 bucks," says George. "What else?"

"Well, there's tires. That's the big ticket item. Probably run you $600 just for one of them big back tires. Anyway, what'er you thinkin', George?"

"I'm thinkin' you're making a mistake. You say Glick offered you $100 for this for scrap?"

"He said that on the phone. My wife said to take it."

"Tell you what. I'm offering you $120 for it right here and now."

Farmer breaks into a smile, rare for him. "Hand me the money and it's a done deal! And I'll be mighty pleased to know somebody's savin' old Ferguson. She was a fine tractor in her time."

"Will be again," argues George as he reaches a greasy hand into his jeans pocket and pulls out a roll of $20 bills. He counts out six and hands them to Farmer.

"Thank you," beams Farmer.

"No thanks needed. I figure with a little effort I can have me a $2,000 tractor."

*   *   *   *   *

"Rats! Now what am I going to do?" complains Ratter as they bump down the road, heading directly toward George the Mechanic's home instead of toward Glick Scrap Company.

"Don't you worry," Ferguson whispers. "If I am going to be worth $2,000, certainly I can find a way to take care of you."

But there was no need for alarm. At George the Mechanic's place Ratter soon discovers plenty of places for a rat to live in luxury.

George sets about the cosmetic work—he cleans, spray paints, and

squirts Gloss Black on the tires to make the rubber look new.

3. Restored

George the Mechanic works fast. That very morning he fills Ferguson's radiator with water, her tires with air, her tank with gas, her crank case with oil, and her transmission with fluid. With his compressor he blasts air in all the cracks and crevices, blowing away many years of dirt, grime, grease, and goo. The rat's nest in the tool box under the hood is scooped out and dumped into the trash. Ratter has long since slipped out of sight into a hole under some wide boards that lean against a wall.

At noon George goes down to the NAPA store and buys a carburetor kit, a new ignition switch, spark plugs and innards for the distributor—points, condenser, and rotor. Back home he installs these items, then hooks up the powerful new battery.

The ripe smell of gasoline fills Ferguson's nose as a new gallon of fuel is pumped into her tank. Then George switches on the ignition. Electricity zings through Ferguson's wires.

"Oh! Oh, aaaaaaah!" she begins to scream, but her voice is drowned by err, err, errrr of the starter, the slow turning of the fan blade, and then the abrupt blasting of valves inside her chest.

"Ker, ker, kerrr-putt ker-putt ker-varoooom!" Ferguson yells, and blue smoke shoots out her rusty tailpipe.

Instead of a gas pedal, Ferguson has a metal stalk on the right side of her steering wheel. Slowly George pulls down on this stalk. "Ker-blam-ity! Ker-blam-ity! Ker-blam-ity!" Louder and louder she goes, and George just lets her run as the blue exhaust gradually becomes less and less blue. Then George sits on her seat, puts her in gear, and drives around the block, testing all four forward gears as well as the reverse.

Everything seems to work! Oh, it feels so wonderful. Wonderful, wonderful, wonderful!

"I'm alive! I'm alive! I'm alive! I'm alive!" Ferguson says this over and over and over again. "I'm alive, I'm alive, I'm alive."

In fourth gear she says this very fast. In third gear she says it more slowly. In second gear she says it thoughtfully. In first gear she says it powerfully.

And in reverse, she says it backward: *"Evil am I."*

By the time George makes it around the block Ferguson's tires are getting soft again, and tiny jets of water spray through the pinholes in the radiator. Fluid also drips from the original leak in the water pump.

"No problem," George mutters to himself. He dumps a bottle of *Stop Leak!* into the radiator. He plugs the gap between the water pump impeller and shaft with high temperature caulk. He squirts a can of *Flat Fix!* into each tire, and then he tops them off with more air from his compressor.

When George drives around the block again, he is pleased to see that the radiator seems to have stopped leaking, the water pump lets out only a tiny, occasional drip, and the tires seem to be holding up just fine.

George next sets about doing the cosmetic work—which takes the better part of a week. He takes off the radiator and air filter hosing and spray-paints them black. He takes off the hood, fenders, and seat and spray-paints them gray. He cleans up the chassis with his power washer and spray-paints it Ferguson gray. Finally, he puts everything back together and squirts more *Gloss Black* on the tires to give them the look of supple, healthy, new rubber.

He then charges up a used battery and hooks it to Ferguson's terminals. As he closes the hood and wipes dirt from his hands, he is heard to chuckle— "Heh heh! And all for less than $200!"

"My, aren't you one lovely beast!" Ratter quips after George goes into the house to call the tractor dealer.

"No, I am not," replies Ferguson. "I am a fraud, that's what I am, and that's *all* I am. But at least I am saved from the scrap pile."

"Fraud or not, I'm stickin' with you," Ratter announces. "This is no place for a rat," and he climbs back up into the tool box under Ferguson's hood to wait and see what the future will bring.

*   *   *   *   *

"Oh! No, no! Don't come over and pick her up!" George is saying into the telephone, "I tell you, she's one reliable old tractor. I'll just drive her on over there to the dealership...."

It is only a one mile drive, but Ferguson is heating up when they arrive. George parks her next to a gimpy-looking Farmall sporting a front-end loader and quickly shuts her off. Then he strides confidently into the office to dicker on a price for his excellent tractor which, as he says, "Is straight off the farm—yessiree—all I done was touch 'er up some and change the oil!"

"You're a cute thing, you are," the old Farmall says in a teasing voice to the freshly painted Ferguson parked next to him. "Nice curve to your fenders…. Park yourself here next to me, honey. We could plow a lot of ground together."

Ferguson tries to ignore him, but Farmall is not to be put off: "Too stuck up to talk to me, are you, Fergy? You can stop the cool act. I know your type— you with the wide front end and the low, sleek look. You've been around!"

"Actually, I've just been saved from the scrap yard," Ferguson informs him. "I am very thankful just to be alive at all." A drop of water falls from her pump to the earth as she speaks.

"There, there now," Farmall scoffs sarcastically. "Don't you go getting sniffy with me. I've two good eyes in my headlights. Nothing gets by me. I know a tractor when I see one. I can tell you've lacked for nothing, dearie. Look at your shiny black air filter hanging so round and delicious like a beautiful earring. Oh yes, and the smooth, thick paint on your hood. You've been coddled, you have—and it's a nice thing to see, I might add. You're a sight for sore eyes."

"The fact is, I lived outdoors on a farm my entire life until just last week," Ferguson corrects him. "I've endured many a cold winter pushing heavy snow. I've known many a long day of hard work in the sweltering sun. I've pulled many a heavy wagon and mowed acres and acres of hay...."

"Smooth! Smooth, lying tongue!" hoots Farmall. "You should write a novel!" He hoists his front-end loader slightly and turns to regard Ferguson in a new light.

"I like you, Fergy. I like your spirit! Tell you what—some of us are having a little party tonight. Just close friends, you know. I could show you a good time. As a matter of fact, Fergy, Doll, tell you what I'm going to—ouch! Ouch!"

Suddenly Farmall twitches painfully and draws his attention back to its usual place—on himself. And there he sees the reason for his pain. Ratter the Rat is chewing on his fan belt—actually biting right through it, and not letting up, either.

"Ouch! Stop that, you rat! Get out of me! Ouch! Get... OUCH!"

But Ratter does not stop until he has chewed clean through the belt. Then he perches on Farmall's front tire and says, "Take that, you bully! And if you keep pestering Fergy, "I'll bite the valve stems off your tires, I will!" But just then George and Dealer come out of the office and ratter dies for cover.

"Not a penny under $2,000," George is saying. "That's my bottom dollar. Ask $2,500, take $2,200, but don't go a penny under $2,000 or I'll lose my shirt!"

"Well, she does look pretty clean," agrees Dealer. "Leave it to you, George, to find the best tractor deal in this county! I'll take my usual commission, of course, but you'll make out. You'll make out just fine. Unless I miss my bet, she'll be sold inside of a month. Here—hop in my truck—I'll give you a lift home."

* * * * *

Two weeks pass. Many people come to look at tractors, but only a few look at either Ferguson or Farmall. Farmall behaves himself a little better, not out of respect for Fergy, but out of fear of losing his valve stems to the sharp teeth of Ratter.

Ratter finds plenty to eat, several good places to sleep, and in general finds ways to make himself right at home.

As for Ferguson, she begins to forget the fragile nature of her repairs. Compared to Farmall she is stunning, indeed. Shoppers look at Farmall, note the potential usefulness of his front-end loader, then turn their attention to Ferguson's lovely paint and black tires.

One customer actually sits in her seat, starts her up, and listens to her valves plunge up and down before shutting her off and walking away.

"That was beautiful," says Farmall. "That was music to my ears. You not only look fabulous—you *are* fabulous. You're a dreamboat. I mean it, Fergy— I'm serious."

"Well, thank you," replies Ferguson. "I do sound pretty good, don't I?"

"Pretty good? You are stunning! You purr like a kitten! It's a secret you just can't keep, Fergy. Everybody here knows it—they all hear you, too. Go ahead, lighten up, babe! Be one of us!"

There is another party that night, and Ferguson goes. But she is always careful to drive herself only in forward gears, never reverse. So the only thing others hear her say—and the only thing she hears herself say—is this: "I'm alive, I'm alive, I'm alive."

4. Sold

The tractor dealership is in shambles come Monday morning. Even the almost-new Ford looks dumpy and his blue paint spattered after the weekend tractor party. Poor old Red Farmall is so tired his front-end loader seems to actually sink into the ground where it rests.

Only Ferguson is awake early, feeling very attractive in the dew and sunshine. "I'm alive, I'm alive! She still chants to herself. "I'm alive! I'm very beautiful! Stunning! Fabulous! Everybody knows it!"

No one but Ferguson notices when the two-door Pontiac Catalina pulls into the dealership. Young Virgil Hartgerink gets out and glances only briefly at the newer tractors, then makes his way toward Red Farmall. First he notices the rusted loader, and the cracked paint, and the generally disheveled grooming—and then he notices the broken fan belt.

"What do you think?" comes the voice of Dealer, who strides out to observe Virgil scrutinizing Farmall.

"How much you asking for the Farmall?"

Not what it's worth. Don't let a little rust fool you. That's one reliable little machine, that."

"How much you asking?"

"Does $2,000 sound like too much?"

"Yes."

"Well, then maybe I could interest you in this slick little Ferguson—born and bred on the farm—well maintained—looks like new. Only asking $2,500 for this beauty."

Virgil turns away from Farmall, rejecting it even as it sleeps with its nose in the ground. He is looking for something reliable, but he knows next to nothing about tractors....

Ferguson is at her best when Dealer sits in her seat, inserts the key in the ignition, gives a tug on the choke and hits the starter. "I'm alive!" she says, right away. After Dealer has her running, he lets Virgil drive her a little bit, shows him how to put the Power Take Off (PTO) in gear, and glows about what a workhorse this cute little job is. Then they turn Ferguson off and go to look at brush hogs, disk harrows, plows, and snowblades.

An hour later Dealer says, "Tell you what I'm going to do—you get the tractor, the snow blade, the old brush hog *and* the disc for $2,900. *And* I'll throw in the upper arm for the three-point hitch."

Virgil counters, "You'll never sell that old re-welded two-bottom plow. Might as well let me take that off your hands, too—for the same price. And I only live about 25 miles from here. Can you throw in free delivery?" As he speaks, he draws his checkbook out of his shirt pocket and looks squarely into Dealer's eyes.

Dealer takes a step backward, sizes up the customer one last time, pulls on his nose with his left hand, and finally replies, "You're taking me to the cleaners, young man—you're taking me to the cleaners. But I'm in a selling mood today—a *selling* mood. I generally don't do free deliveries, not as a rule. But for you—shucks! It's a deal."

"Okay," says Virgil. He writes out a check for the whole amount, watches Dealer load the newly purchased farm equipment onto a trailer, then climbs back into his old Pontiac and drives away.

Ratter scrambles into his usual spot under Ferguson's hood at the last possible moment. As they move out the driveway Ferguson shouts to her tractor friends, "Good bye! I'm alive! I'm beautiful! And I have a new home!"

Ferguson's new home is on a curve at the end of a road in a quiet subdivision. There is a nice house with a garage, and behind the house crouches a row of piled-up stones dividing the back yard from a large field. The stones remain in the fence row, but the fence is long since gone.

Huge oak trees grow in a line where the fence once was. Grapevines creep over the stones, and beyond the stones tall, tall weeds stand higher than Ferguson as far as she can see.

Ferguson is parked in those weeds along with the other pieces of farm equipment. There is no barn, no shed, no shelter of any kind—just big trees that block the sun except in the early morning.

"What kind of farm is this?" demands Ratter. "No chickens, no pigs, no corn crib, no hay mow, no nuthin'! Crummy place for a rat."

Ferguson looks around and shivers even though it is warm. "I don't know. And I certainly don't like the idea of being left out here in these high weeds. This Virgil Hartgerink man...."

"What an odd name! scoffs Ratter. "Let's call him VH for short."

"Good idea. Well, this VH fellow, you don't think he expects me to plow down all these weeds, do you?"

Ratter glances toward Re-weld the Two-Bottom Plow, thick with rust, and ventures, "Then what's the plow for?"

"Oh my, oh my!" sniffs Ferguson. She shivers again. "I really don't think I can pull that plow. It looks so heavy—*so* heavy. And this ground, this isn't at all *sandy* soil. This looks to be mostly clay and rocks. Oh, what am I to do?"

"You're a tractor, ain't you?" insists Ratter. "Isn't plowin' what you're made for? And you're such a *beautiful* and such an *alive* tractor! Farmall said so, and you said so yourself. So what's the big deal?"

"Oh, but you don't understand! You can't understand! Plowing is such dreadfully hard work. Even when I was new it was hard work. And now I am not fit for such work. I know I *look* nice, but I'm *not* nice inside. Oh! I can say I'm alive easily enough, when other tractors are standing around looking at my new paint. However, my new owner will be terribly disappointed when he discovers what I'm really like on the inside...."

"Ease up on it, will ya?" scowls Ratter. "You underestimate yourself, Fergy. George the Mechanic saved you, didn't he? And he's a mechanic, right? And if he thinks you're fit for service, then just go out there an' do the job!"

"Oh yes, he saved me from destruction all right. But I am *not* fit for service. I am *not*. Oh, whatever will Virgil Hartgerink think of me now? And he spent all that money to buy me...."

"Come, come," retorts Ratter. "VH thinks he got himself a right good deal!"

"I'm afraid he'll find out better soon enough," Ferguson admits.

Ratter perches on Ferguson's seat and announces, "Well, never you mind, Fergy. If VH has the money to buy you, maybe he has the money to...." At the moment the house door slams. VH walks toward them carrying a five gallon can of gas. Ratter dives for cover in the weeds and never finishes his sentence. VH pours the gas into Ferguson's tank, checks her water and oil, and switches on the ignition.

"I'm... I'mmmm..." says Ferguson.

VH pulls out her choke.

I... I... I'm... I'm... I'mmm..." Ferguson says again.

41

VH checks to make sure the power take-off is out of gear. He double-checks that the transmission is in neutral. He waits a few seconds. Then he tries again.

"I'm... I'm... I'mmm... **I'm a... a... I'm alive!**" Black smoke shoots out her exhaust pipe. She rattles and shakes, almost stalls, and then—as VH pulls down on her throttle—she begins saying rapidly, "...but I don't wanna plow don't wanna plow don't wanna plow don't wanna plow...."

Ratter watches from a safe distance as VH backs Ferguson toward Re-Weld the Two-Bottom Plow. For this brief trip in reverse Ferguson puts her hand over her mouth to garble the message she speaks, and Ratter smiles to hear, "Elvis, my my! Elvis, my my!" instead of "*Evil am I.*"

Using the three-point hitch, VH connects the plow, then engages the power take-off. Pulling the PTO lever up, he watches pensively as Ferguson valiantly hoists the plow into the air.

"Feels good, Ferguson," says Re-weld the Plow. "Feels real good to be hooked up to someone like you again. I don't look like much with all this rust, but I'm stout as ever."

"You sure are," gasps Ferguson. "Wow, you've got a lot of iron in you."

42

"Yes, and I can roll this clay like pie dough! Not only that, but pull me across this field a few times, Ferguson, and I'll begin to really shine! This rust will wear off in no time, you'll see. I can work as hard as the day I was made, I can."

"I wish it were so easy for me," grunts Ferguson. "But I've just been saved from the scrap heap. I look nice enough, but there is so much more that I need...." She can say no more. VH has put her in first gear, yanked the throttle to full speed, and is slowly letting out the clutch. The plow will hit the dirt any minute now, and Ferguson simply cannot talk and work at the same time.

They drive along the end of the field as VH looks for an old dead furrow to plow into. Locating one, he positions Ferguson's right tires in the low spot and carefully lowers the plow to just touch the ground. Re-weld begins to easily peel over a shallow swatch of weeds and sod, revealing damp brown soil and startled earthworms and insects.

Goldfinches feeding on thistle gone to seed rise in waves of winged sunlight. Grasshoppers knocked from towering ragweed land on Ferguson's hood, then spring off in all directions. Dust knocked from plants by Ferguson's tires and Re-weld's cutting rise in a steady cloud.

"Eeeps!" peeps a tiny voice. "You've destroyed my cozy nest!"

"Sorry!" booms Re-weld to the astonished, grayish brown mouse, so rudely awakened from an afternoon nap. "Quick, jump on my back and I'll take you to a safer place!"

The little Church Mouse leaps and manages to cling to a clump of weeds dragging behind the plow. Her pointed snout twitches nervously, her round black eyes pop from her brow, and her thin pink tail streams out behind her.

"You won't last long on that clump," advises Re-weld. "Climb up on my frame."

"Eeeps!" the mouse peeps again, and with her clever fingers and toes she scurries into a comfortable, out-of-sight position on the plow.

"There are stones where I was parked," explains Re-weld. "When we go back there you will find many nice tunnels just your size—a good place to build a safer nest that even I can't smash."

After only one trip down the length of the field, Ferguson begins to sneeze. The plow is just a couple inches into the sod and hardly moving any dirt at all as VH experiments with the PTO lever and tests the capacities of his new tractor.

On the return trip VH lowers the plow another inch or two into the soil. Ferguson's sneezing becomes more pronounced, she starts to cough, and by the time she is half way back she is running a fever.

VH tugs harder on the throttle, trying to get more *oomph* out of Ferguson. Then he lowers Re-weld the full eight inches into the soil—the proper depth for plowing.

"Ugh!" shrieks Ferguson. Tremors run through her entire body. She grinds quickly to a halt.

Alarmed, VH promptly stomps on the clutch. Ferguson is instantly motionless. He then takes her out of gear and slowly lets up the clutch to raise the plow out of the soil. Church Mouse clings to the frame, peering down from what seems a dizzying height, and holds on with grim resolve.

Re-weld looks himself over with satisfaction. The rust is not clear gone yet, but flecks of shiny iron gleam through in places. With a few more passes around the field he will have begun to look handsome indeed.

Ferguson gasps and gasps. It feels so good to stand still. It would feel even better to be turned off. She desperately needs a rest. Green tears spurt from her now boiling radiator, and all four tires are beginning to sag.

Virgil Hartgerink gets off the tractor, walks around it twice, kicks the sagging tires, then quickly jumps back on. "Good grief!" he yells at the tractor over the rattling that now issues from Ferguson's throat, "You're not fit for any real work! I'll be lucky to get you back to the shop, that's what."

VH lowers Re-weld the Plow a full eight inches into the soil. "Ugh!" shrieks Ferguson. Tremors run through her entire body. She grinds quickly to a halt.

5. The Cost of Discipleship

Virgil Hartgerink is not exactly shouting into the telephone, but he isn't exactly whispering, either. "That's exactly what I said," he breaths through clenched teeth. "Make it right or I'll void that check and you'll come back and pick up your farm junk or it'll rust forever in my field."

Dealer is used to such customers. He speaks calmly. He reassures VH that there must be some mistake. He says it is a surprise to him that Ferguson isn't just the very finest tractor he has ever sold.

In the end, he recommends a gentleman who he says is perhaps the finest tractor mechanic this side of Timbuktu. He offers to personally pick up the cost of that first service call. "Yessir," he affirms, "If George the Mechanic can't fix your tractor, then it can't be fixed. I'll personally explain the problem to him and send him right on over."

George arrives to find Ferguson cooling down under the oak trees near the row of rocks. Re-weld rests behind her, still coupled to her three-point hitch.

The mechanic expertly removes the hood by twisting apart two large bolts, has the radiator off in a matter of minutes, and chatters continually about Ferguson's various positive qualities as he works.

"I had a tractor like this once," he allowed. "The TO-20 is one of the finest tractors ever built. This wide front end, now, you want that in a tractor. And when it comes to repairs, nothing's easier than working on one of these Fergusons. Take this radiator, which you need to have re-cored. I know a fella can have it fixed like new for under a hundred bucks.

"Yup, just what I figured. See this here leak from the impeller shaft? Means the water pump's shot. These pumps tend to go out due to the fan belt tension. It costs $65 for a new water pump. You buy the pump and I'll do you a favor and install it at no cost to you, since Dealer said he was picking up the tab on this job.

"Well, looky here! This carburetor's been totally rebuilt. They did nice work, too. This old girl has one of them gravity feed carburetors—should give you trouble-free service for years. Even has a new gas filter. Somebody took real good care of this old girl, looks like.

"And yer electrical system looks very good, but I'd recommend putting in a new battery. You know farmers. They tend to use a battery way past its useful life—always keeping them hooked up to a charger and what not.

"One thing though, I hope you didn't pay a dollar over $3,000 for this tractor, but I reckon it'd be a good investment even at that price.

"She'll be needing new tires—no doubt you noticed that before you bought it. Now, *there's* a hefty investment—probably run you $700 all around. But without 'em you're likely to waste an entire day on a flat when you could be working. I say, fix it right the first time.

"See this here black canister next to the battery? That there's one of the cleverest air filtering inventions in the whole world. Nowadays you pay an arm and a leg to buy a new paper filter every time you turn around. This one you just wash out from time to time, and then refill the oil reservoir to the level indicated, see? Never cost you a penny to operate.

"Your ignition switch is shot. See how I haf'ta wiggle this wire to get any juice on my volt meter? No problem, though. I got a spare switch right here in my tool box. Might as well install 'er right this minute—ain't doin' nobody no good sittin' there in my tool box!"

One minute Virgil Hartgerink feels thrilled by the excellent investment he's made in this fine antique tractor, and the next minute he feels devastated by the mounting dollar signs in George the Mechanic's eyes. VH is first proud to have a hand in restoring one of the world's truly classic tractors, then troubled by the possibility that he is making a huge mistake. He is happy at the prospect of having a reliable machine to work his field, yet discouraged that said machine cannot be relied on for any real work.

But George is saying, "I was looking at *new* tractors the other day. Sometimes it's tempting to think a new tractor's the way to go. Well, don't you believe it! Do you know what they're getting for new tractors these days? I mean just for *little* tractors? Would you believe $15,000 or so?! And that's without any equipment at all. That's without any fuel in the tank. And then if something should happen to go wrong you have to pay $65 an hour for a mechanic in white gloves with a PhD in electronics to fix the lousy rig! Now then, if this was my tractor I'd do something about this transmission...."

*　*　*　*　*

"What good is having a tractor if I can't use it for anything?" is Virgil Hartgerink's final question to himself.

"No good at all," he answers himself, and once again he reaches for his checkbook.

*　*　*　*　*

Right there under the oak tree, with everyone watching, Ferguson is stripped practically naked. George has already removed her hood and radiator and water pump. Now he removes her wheels, rotten tires and all, and hoists them onto the back of his truck. Then her oil pan is removed and George sets Virgil to work cleaning out the gooey black scum caked in there. They take off the air filter, blast it clean with a compressor, and fill the reservoir with clean oil. The battery is removed and George allows as how he'll get rid of it and deliver a new one when he comes back.

They take off her starter. "It'll need rebuilding," explains George. "I know a motor man down in

Litchfield who can outfit this with new bushings and have it humming real sweet."

They take off Ferguson's gas tank, eventually decide to overhaul the entire engine, and ultimately hoist *that* onto George's truck. "It'll be easier to work on in the shop," comes the explanation.

They take away this, they take away that. They just keep tearing her down. Pieces continue to disappear until Ferguson no longer looks very much like a tractor. Her parts, like giant puzzle pieces scrambling loosely in a box, are tossed helter-skelter into the back of George the Mechanic's truck.

* * * * *

Darkness falls. George the Mechanic drives away. Virgil Hartgerink retreats into his house. Ratter the Rat, with no proper place to lodge himself on Ferguson's gaunt frame, slinks away up the road in search of more congenial accommodations. He never even says goodbye.

Re-weld hunkers down behind what remains of Ferguson. He is capable as ever, but stranded without the leadership he needs to prepare the rich soil for planting.

Church Mouse has long since ducked into the rock pile to evaluate her prospects. Now, as a sliver of moon rises in the east, she begins scurrying about in search of dry leaves or grass to make a nest.

"I'm sorry again," volunteers Re-weld to the mouse. "The thing I like least about my work is the way I upend the homes of so many harmless field folks...."

"Eeeps!" says Church Mouse. "Your big voice scared me! But do not make such a big thing of it. This world eeps not my home."

"It isn't? But certainly you are here, just the same."

"Yes, but it eeps just a place for now, not forever. I can make do with just any mouthful of mulch. We church mice are noted for that."

"Wouldn't you more accurately fit the classification of *field* mouse?"

"Eeeps! Not at all! I used to live in a church—an old stone church. But they tore it down and I have wandered ever so far since that time."

"Then a stone pile such as you now have must seem familiar," suggests Re-weld. There is nothing he enjoys after a day of hard work than to converse with whatever creatures live nearby where he happens to be parked for a night. It has been some years since such an opportunity has come his way, and he finds Church Mouse most charming.

"Eeeps! Yes! The stone pile is lovely as a cathedral! And plenty of room under there for an extended family...." Church Mouse talks freely as she busily darts about gathering nesting material, liberally sprinkling conversation with her habitual eeps and squeaks. She pauses frequently to gaze up with her round, black eyes, ever wary of hawks, snakes, and cats.

"I am glad I was able to save you," says Re-weld.

"Eeeps! But you haven't! I've already been saved, saved, saved to the uttermost! Hallelujah! Through and through! And if I may say so, that is what your tractor friend needs."

"But she *has* been saved," insists Re-weld. "Wouldn't you say so, Ferguson?"

There is no reply, for Ferguson cannot speak. Silenced by many missing parts and broken beyond recognition, she can only listen with the two ear-like fenders that loom hugely into the sky, all out of proportion in the absence of her large rear wheels.

"Eeeps!" chirps Church Mouse. "She can't talk. She can't move. She has no power...."

Yes, thinks Ferguson. *I am empty. I am nothing. I am disgraced, for to be without power is the ultimate disgrace for any tractor. All the evil that I feared has come upon me.*

"Hold it, hold it," Re-weld admonishes the mouse. "She has indeed been saved, and that is certainly a noble beginning...."

"Eeeps! Yes! A noble beginning, but only just a start. She must not only be saved, but also *sanctified,* eeepspecially if she is ever to be of any real use to her master."

Church Mouse, thinks Ferguson, *I know you mean well, but you don't make any sense to me at all.*

"I wouldn't know what you mean with your fancy language," RE-weld is saying. "But I clearly remember the day I broke like a twig between your teeth. It was then that a master craftsman took his torch to me.

"Yes, mouse, I went through heat that would instantly incinerate your juicy little body. He melted me. He bent me. He beat on me as the sparks flew upward. He grafted in new reinforcement metal. He made me into a tool that can do the work of two plows.

"Being re-welded wasn't at all pleasant at the time, but it has made me who I am, and I wouldn't exchange what I have been through for anything in the world."

"Eeeps!" cries the mouse. "You are saying exactly what I mean! You have yourself been set aside for a special purpose, and this is precisely what Ferguson needs…."

"Yes," Re-weld smiles. "And I believe we can leave it to her master to see to that."

Yes, thinks Ferguson. *I am empty. I am nothing. I am disgraced, for to be without power is the ultimate disgrace for any tractor. All the evil that I feared has come upon me.*

6. Fit For Service

Re-weld the Two-Bottom Plow and the other farm implements sit on the ground with Ferguson for seven days and seven nights. No one says a word. They all see how great her suffering is.

Ferguson also sits in silence, for she has no choice. Her voice box is gone, her tool box is gone, her gear box is gone, her gas tank is gone, her wheels are gone, her engine is gone.

She cannot talk, but she has plenty of time to think. She thinks back to what Ratter the Rat said about Old Orange, long ago back there on the farm, and she understands how he must have felt to be dismembered. One of Old Orange's fenders has become a sled. His front wheels serve on a manure spreader. His flywheel is now a boat anchor. His seat continues to bring comfort bolted so firmly to a stump down by the fishing pond.

At least Old Orange's parts are of some use. Better to be dismembered and put into various types of service than to be completely *dismissed* as utterly *useless.* Ferguson would weep bitter tears, but her radiator is gone, and she is unable even to cry.

*   *   *   *   *

Around high noon the following week Virgil Hartgerink comes out the back door of his house and walks contemplatively toward his recently acquired collection of farm equipment. He wears work boots, heavy jeans, and leather gloves.

He glances over his as yet untried equipment—the disk, the brush hog, and the show blade. He touches Re-weld approvingly with his gloved hand. Then he turns a look of consternation toward the skeletal remains of Ferguson.

"Old girl," he says quietly, "you have cost me dearly. It has cost me as much to make you fit for service as it cost to buy you in the first place. See that you live up to my expectations."

But I'm not fit for service, Ferguson wants to argue. *You have destroyed what little future there was for me. And what do you mean, "has cost"? Have you already done something for me that I don't know about?*

No one can hear her thoughts, of course, but Re-weld is thinking along similar lines. Glancing confidently at Ferguson he says, "When someone is willing to pay the high price, and when that cost *has already been paid*, you can expect great things to happen suddenly."

No sooner has he spoken when the air is split by the screeching brakes of George the Mechanic's truck. He bounds out, shakes Virgil's hand enthusiastically, and leaps back to the truck to lower the tailgate:

"Yessiree Mr. Hartgerink," he announces, "We're ready to put the old tractor-puzzle back together, we are! Took a ton of rust off these wheel rims, we did, repainted them, and mounted brand spanking new rubber and tubes all around. Loaded them, too, for traction. You're set for 20 years or I miss my bet!"

Using a special machine designed for moving heavy objects, one by one he maneuvers the large rear wheels into position and mounts them under Ferguson's elephant-like fender ears. The smaller two he installs on the front axle.

Ferguson cannot believe her eyes. No cracks or breaks in these tires! And such a lot of tread! There are still little black rubber pimples everywhere, as if they have just come out of a mold. How they grip her rims! And how tall and firm they feel. *Gracious me oh my, my, my!* Ferguson wants to scream with the thrill of it, but she still can't talk.

Then George wheels out a cart, and with the help of a stranger who has come along, they transport what looks like a factory new engine toward Ferguson. "We did it all!" he exclaims. "Did a valve job, adjusted the rocker arms to the new tappets— made her purrr like a kitten. You'll have to listen twice to know she's running." This is not strictly true, Ferguson is sure, because she does not remember purring like a kitten even on the day she was first made, but hearing him say so makes her smile like a kitten.

The two men work quickly to mount the engine and reconnect the transmission housing. Shiny silver bolts and nuts, new electrical wires and clean water tubes, rubber bushings and fresh gaskets, a completely new water pump, and the radiator has a new core that can hold her own even in the hottest conditions.

On one of his trips between truck and tractor, George the Mechanic's helper carries over a 650 amp battery that has never seen service. Says he to

61

George, "First time you hit the starter now, she'll think she's been electrocuted!"

The starter itself sports bright coppery innards and a snug feeling that surprises Ferguson when its bolts are tightened.

They fit the gear assembly into place and there is not one extra little bit of looseness between Ferguson's motor, her camshaft, her gear box, her differential, her PTO, or her axles. She is finely crafted machinery. Redone according to factory specifications. Rebuilt by the book.

George installs new brake linings while his helper remounts the gas tank and hood. Virgil, who has been watching all the activity with considerable curiosity and enjoyment, now goes away, soon to return once again with his five-gallon gas can.

The sun is dropping into the western skies and it is getting on toward supper time when George makes one last twist on a bolt, then grunts through a very sweaty, dirty face, "That oughta do it."

They pour six quarts of new motor oil into Ferguson's engine. They pour two large containers of clean hydraulic fluid into her gear box. They pour sparkling green antifreeze into her radiator, mixing in just the right amount of cold, clean water. Finally,

Virgil pours the five gallons of gasoline into Ferguson's tank.

Then George the Mechanic reaches into his pocket, pulls out a shiny new key, and hands it to Virgil. He does this without saying a word, for he is enjoying the suspense of the moment. He is also busy searching his mind to be sure everything has been done exactly as the shop manual specifies.

The towering oak trees overhead hold their breath. Church Mouse pops out of her hole and stands on hind legs. Re-weld shifts his weight from one moldboard bottom to the other. George the Mechanic and his helper lean back and fold their arms across their chests.

Virgil Hartgerink swings himself up into Ferguson's seat. He inserts the key into the ignition and switches it to the right. He tugs on the choke and presses on the starter.

"Tha... than... than..." says the starter. It is a completely new sound.

Virgil switches off the ignition and glances at George, who shrugs and says, "The new gas line's still empty—gotta get fuel to the carburetor before she'll run. Hit 'er again!"

"Tha… than… than…" says the starter, "tha… than… than…."

Suddenly Ferguson understands, and quickly takes up the theme introduced by the starter. "Tha… than… thank… thank-you thank-you thank-you thank-you thank-you thank-you thank-you."

This is all she says. It is a surprisingly quiet sound for a tractor. As George had promised, Virgil has to "listen twice" to be sure she is running. But he looks back and sees clear exhaust shooting from the tail pipe.

They attach Re-weld to the three-point hitch, and when Virgil engages the PTO the plow almost leaps into the air. He advances the throttle and Ferguson keeps saying the same thing, not louder, just faster: "Thank-you thank-you thank-you thank-you thank-you."

"Go ahead!" says George, not having to yell over the sound of Ferguson. "Run down the field and back—see if she can plow now!"

Virgil nods, puts Ferguson in gear, and drives to the point in the field where he left off when first he had purchased the tractor. With growing confidence he drops Ferguson into first gear, pulls the throttle to full speed, and lowers the plow a full eight or ten inches into the ground.

"Swoooosh!" rolls the soil.

"Yes!" yells Re-weld.

"How do you like this?" asks Ferguson, glancing back over her shoulder with the widest grin Re-weld has ever seen on a tractor.

"I like it," Re-weld replies. "But I thought you said you can't talk and work at the same time!"

"But now I don't feel like I'm working to excess," is the happy tractor's reply. "Yes, this is stout work, but it is the work I was made to do. I feel wonderful!"

Ferguson continues across the field, singing as she works, "Made-to-do thank-you made-to-do thank-you made-to-do thank-you made-to-do...."

*　　*　　*　　*　　*

Four years later, Ferguson stands in her usual shady spot under the oaks, next to the rocks. The many children of Church Mouse scamper about at her feet. Re-weld and the several other tools with whom she works so closely are constant companions.

Snow blade rests comfortably, indulging in a bit of rust, knowing it will be some time yet before she is put to steady use once again. Mower rests gratefully, having put in a very long day behind Ferguson just yesterday. Re-weld hunkers nearby, looking forward to the fall plowing in preparation for winter wheat or a rye cover crop.

Virgil Hartgerink often joins his mechanical friends there in the fence row. Just now he leans comfortably against Ferguson's left rear tire, chewing on a stem of grass and gazing out on the fields, which are ripe and ready for harvest.

"Well," Virgil suddenly says out loud. "An important phone call came through today. Everything's been decided. You, Ferguson," and he thunks her fender affectionately, "are on your way to Mexico to be a missionary. Our church has a ranch down there that needs plowing and planting and harvesting, and I think you are just the creature for the job. It's hot, desert work, to be sure, that's what. But you have never lost your cool, not since that first day before you were remade. A truck will be coming for you tomorrow."

This is not the first time Ferguson has heard of such a thing. Somehow, she is not at all surprised. Nor is she unprepared. Why, just that morning she had taught an important lesson to the cluster of Church

Mouse children. Re-weld overheard her say, as he had heard her say many times before, "Being saved is a wonderful experience, to be sure, my little ones. But it is only a beginning—only a beginning. And it can tend toward pride and vanity and false confidence.

"Being made fit for service may count for more in the long haul, for only then do you have the power to live as you were meant to live. Since that day I was rebuilt I have never been ashamed, for I have always been able to do everything my master expects a tractor like me to do.

"I often think of Harry Ferguson, the genius who invented me. I think back to that day I rolled off the assembly line where I was created. And I know that if he were to see me at work today, he would smile well. He would surely say, 'Well done, good and faithful tractor.'

"Now then, you are mice and not tractors, and your purpose is entirely different from mine. But surely your maker expects nothing less of you—you cute little mice children!"

And it is true. In all her years of toil, Ferguson has served with distinction. At every opportunity she teaches others the same lesson she practiced first on the Church Mice children.

And by the time when most folks expected her to retire, she only slowed down, or carried lighter loads. And everywhere she goes, both her song and bubbly example are always heard and seen: "Made-to-do thank-you made-to-do thank-you made-to-do thank-you made-to-do...."

—The End—

Section II: Selected Ruminations

Ferguson "wrote" an advice column for *Free Methodist World Mission People* magazine from 1992-1995. She greatly enjoyed this assignment and was known to mix considerable humor with her thoughtful guidance.

Ferguson's desire was to see these collected ruminations published. In this text her every stated desire is being carried out to its fullest extent.

Problem—Ferguson can't actually write! Hence, I call them "ruminations"—things I heard her mulling over of an evening out under the oak tree in the fence row.

As an underground writer, I began scribbling down her thoughts. When I came out of my hole to show her the results, she seemed very pleased, even though she cannot read a word of Molish.

One day I took a substantial risk and left a sheaf of bark containing my text where the Reverend Doctor Daniel V. Runyon might happen upon it. He is a very close friend of VH and was in the habit of stopping by from time to time to help with chores.

Ferguson and I both held our collective breaths when we saw him drop his wood-chopping axe, sit down on the stump he was about to split, and carefully scrutinize my penmanship. He pushed his hat back, scratched his head near the temple, and began to half-out-loud translate the Molish into the more pleasing tones of his own native tongue.

When he returned a day later, the axe still lay where it had fallen, and Dr. Dan did not pick it up again. Instead, he searched the area, found another sheaf I had brought out, and hurried back home to type some more.

My leaving of the bark-scribbled ruminations of Ferguson and Runyon's translating of them became routine. Needless to say, Ferguson and I were more than pleased, yet astonished when, one afternoon, he came unexpectedly.

He was accompanied by an art student then studying at Spring Arbor University. This fellow, a Mr. Scott Auch, showed remarkable talent as he created pictures of Ferguson, the mice, and *Yours Truly* by merely making ink dots on his paper. *Stipple*, it is called.

Now you know the never-before-published mystery of how *Ferguson's Tractor-biography and*

Selected Ruminations came to be. In my vanity, I truly wish you could read it in the earthy tones of Molish. But all is not lost and much gained in translation. Hence, I hope that you delight to read what Ferguson delighted to think and I to scribble.

Benjamin Titus Mole, Ph.D.

This World's Wisdom

Dear Ferguson:

Thank you for sharing the story of how God prepared you for missionary service. You have helped me to see that such a way to spend a life is the natural and spontaneous result of humble obedience and a mature faith.

I always used to hold missionaries up on a pedestal as super saints. Now I see they are regular people who just keep on saying "yes" to God's leading, and God leads them into missions.

In my own life I am beginning to realize that I am not good at saying "yes" to God. I am good at telling him what **I** want, but not so good at finding out what **He** wants.

For quite a few years I have been explaining to God the many reasons why obedience to His call is out of the question for me. Your story has made me wonder, how can I be sure that not being a missionary is God's plan for me?

—Wendy in Iowa

Dear Wendy,

There is a story I should have told in my tractor-biography, but Dr. Mole chopped it out because parts of it are rather gruesome. Now I am going to tell that story anyway, because it will help you understand how God's wisdom is better than the world's.

It happened in Mexico rather early during my first term. Young Pablo had learned to drive me and was mowing a five- or six-acre field. Round and round that field we went, and with each time around, the patch of tall grass became smaller and smaller and smaller.

A family of rabbits was living in that tall grass, a mother and two young bunnies. One bunny was strong, and proud, and could run very fast, The other bunny was a runt, not very brave, and quite clumsy. When he ran, his rear end bounced sideways and his back feet tripped on his front ones. He was a poor excuse for a rabbit.

Well, the noise of my motor and the whirring of the mower blade were equally frightening to both bunnies, but they responded in different ways. The weak bunny crouched in terror and trembled. The strong bunny kicked up his heels and shot along in front of me like a furry cruise missile. Then he would dive into the tallest grass to hide as I passed by.

Finally, there was just one more long narrow strip of tall grass to mow and then all the field would be laid bare—a very uncomfortable place for a rabbit to find herself. So the weak little bunny quietly hopped out into the open and gave herself up, right out there in the short grass where any fox or hawk could quickly snatch her away.

Meanwhile, Mr. Strong Bunny followed every wild rabbit instinct in the book—running fast, darting unpredictably, and generally putting on an impressive show of athletic acumen and worldly wisdom. Because he always insisted on staying in the tall grass, the inevitable finally happened. On my last pass across the field that proud rabbit collapsed in exhaustion, was crushed by my front tire, and utterly destroyed by the sharp, whirling, steel blades of the mower.

Pablo never saw the strong, "wise" rabbit, nor did he feel that creature's body disintegrate under the machinery. But when he noticed the frightened bunny that surrendered its life in the open field, he stopped me, leaped to the ground in delight, and took off his shirt for use in collecting that furry little ball to himself.

We fed and cared for that rabbit, named her Scooter, and after a few weeks set her free. But she chose to live nearby in a burrow under a log, and actually became friends with a dog that would normally be her natural enemy.

This experience reminded me of something Paul wrote to the people he loved in Corinth: *Do not deceive yourselves. If any one of you thinks he is wise by the standards of this age, he should become a "fool" so that he may become wise. For the wisdom of this world is foolishness in God's sight. As it is written: "He catches the wise in their craftiness"; and again, "The Lord knows that the thoughts of the wise are futile"* (1 Cor. 3:18-20).

Wendy, you are behaving like that strong rabbit. If you keep telling God what to do instead of asking Him what to do and then obeying His instructions, you will ultimately destroy yourself. Instead, please join me and the Apostle Paul in being a fool for Jesus' sake.

Do this and I promise that you can live longer and better and happier, both in this life and in the life to come. The only way you can be sure that **not** being a missionary is God's plan for you is to obey Him fully, and then try to keep track of all the things He does **not** do in your life!

Do Missionaries Get Mad?

Dear Ferguson,

I read your tractor-biography when it first appeared in the mission magazine, and I really felt sorry for the hard life you lived. I noticed that most of your hardships came along **before** you became a missionary! Is that normal?

Also, I am wondering—I have often thought maybe I should be a missionary, but something stops me. Although I have been a Christian for many years and am trying to obey God in every way, I have a bad temper that I simply cannot seem to conquer. And if I can't even live up to my own expectations, how can I ever serve the Lord or be an example to others?

—*Hot in Washington*

Dear Hot,

Your first question is much easier, so let me answer that one first. *Everyone* has hardships in life. We all have accidents, grow old, break down, and experience the usual wear and tear you would expect, just because we're alive. So I would have to say that, yes, my pre-missionary experience was pretty normal.

However, please do not jump to the conclusion that God will take away all your troubles when you commit yourself to a life of obedience. More likely, your troubles will take on a different nature. *Before* obedience, the hardships of life are confined to the ordinary aspects of living in a world ruined by Satan.

After obedience, the hardships took on less importance for me as I experienced the truth Jesus shared in Matthew 6:25-33: *Do not worry about your life, what you will eat or drink; or about your body, what you will wear. Is not life more important than food, and the body more important than clothes? For the pagans run after all these things, and your heavenly Father knows that you need them. But seek first His kingdom and His righteousness, and all these things will be given to you as well.*

God has proven Himself to be just like a good farmer who knows better than to put gas in my radiator or water in my transmission.

Fighting God's Battles

My experience is that *after* obedience, my troubles tend toward being spiritual warfare. Satan does not want me to be content and obedient and cooperating with God, so he throws grenades in my path. My only way to fight back is through prayer and faithfulness, so that the Holy Spirit will go before me and act as a sort of mine sweeper.

In other words, when we start fighting God's battles for Him, He starts fighting our battles for us. As soon as we pull back and return to fighting our own battles, we step into spiritual grenades much too big for us, and we get blown up into itty bitty pieces.

For you (and now I am coming to the second part of your question), these grenades come in the form of anger. For others, they come in the form of old, bad habits such as drugs, alcohol, or sexual activities that God rejects. Whatever it is, most people have *something* that defeats them and forces them back to reliance on Almighty God.

In spite of your anger, I urge you to start serving God where you are. Work in your church or community with whatever gifts you have—music, teaching, leading a small group, doing visitation, serving on a board, taking meals to a shut-in, mowing the lawn—whatever.

Thinking of the Wrong Example

And when your anger surfaces (as it most surely will), thank the Lord for it, because your anger continually reminds you of your need for God. And then, give your anger over to Him.

Next (and this is the hard part), share your problem with someone you trust. Ask this person to do two things: Pray for you often, and hold you accountable to talking with you on a regular basis about how you are doing.

In this way you can both serve the Lord and be an example to others—not an example of perfection—but certainly an example of obedience and humility.

As for whether you will then be qualified to be a missionary, that depends on many other things. However, as time passes, the Lord will make your missionary call clear to you if that is what he wants you to do. Meanwhile, you will be where God wants you to be, and that is certainly a step in the right direction.

Mileage Plus

Dear Ferguson,

Okay, like, I was talking with my girlfriends, see, and we agreed I should text you.

It's like, well, we're really into travel, okay? And we think missionaries are the greatest. 'Cause, like, they get to go so many places! They see the world!

It's like, missionaries are always gettin' on an' off airplanes, like the president of the United States! What a life! You know what I mean?

Okay, so missionaries don't get paid much, and they're always seeing poverty all the time—but I bet they get used to that. I bet it probably doesn't bother them after a while.

Teaching about God all the time can't be such a bad thing either. See, having gone to Sunday school all our lives, it's like we got the Bible and religion pretty well down!

After you've read the Bible and learned all the songs and how to take an offering and all—I mean, like, what more is there? We could probably even learn to baptize people and do the Lord's Supper and everything!

And serving communion. That's totally easy—I helped with that once.

So we wanna know, is this attraction to missions a call from God, or what? Can we, like take this to the bank?

—Tricia

Dear Tricia,

No.

Homosexual Clergy

Dear Ferguson:

My pastor is gay and says God does not discriminate, so neither should we. He has a live-in lover man and they have been together for 16 years. Now that the Supreme Court has said it's ok, they are talking of getting married.

He says for him to be homosexual is just like for a black person to be black—it's genetic and there's nothing he can do about it. It's not sin; it's just him.

I have read the Bible and I don't think he's right about this. And if he can get something this important so wrong, how can I trust him when it comes to understanding other parts of the Bible?

I don't want to judge him, but I also don't want to be deceived by him. What should I do?

—Straight and Narrow

Dear Straight,

Before my conversion I lived on a farm with chickens. Cock the rooster dominated the roost and both protected and fertilized hens. Gwenn the Road Island Red routinely raised a clutch of baby chicks.

When chicks come out of the shell, they are vulnerable to any snake or rodent living nearby. Gwenn kept them close and warm as they grew feathers and became large enough to fend for themselves. Life was precarious. Predators lurked.

You are like a baby chick!—surrounded by powers intent on destroying you. You need a spiritual mother like Gwenn the Hen to warm you, and a spiritual father like Cock the Rooster to drive away the snakes.

In other countries missionaries confront witch doctors who embody the powers of Satan. Sorry to say, your pastor is one such snake—a wolf in sheep's clothing. Have nothing more to do with him. Find another church. Run for your life.

Satan prowls like a lion, seeking to devour. The world you live in is hostile to your spiritual survival and will surely destroy you. Deceived themselves, they cannot help but deceive others.

Run, don't walk, to a church that refuses to compromise the clear teachings of the Bible, regardless of the social pressure to do otherwise. Your life depends on it.

How to Pick Your Dead Furrow

Dear Ferguson:

My wife and I are bored. Not with each other!—but with life. I am 24 and she is 23. We met in college and we were married after I graduated and got a job. Now she has graduated too, and she teaches school.

Just three years ago we were all nervous about our uncertain future. We talked about how for her to get a teaching job we might have to move to Alaska or something exotic like that. Now the future is here, and it is boring. We have two incomes, two cars, and a first-class apartment. We could buy a house.

My in-laws keep bugging us about starting a family. Nothing like a screaming bundle of dirty diaper to cancel out the boredom! But we're just not ready for that.

We're both Christians and really want to honor God with our lives. We're involved in our church and try to be a good influence at our places of work. But it seems there should be more to life than just locking into this groove for the next 40 years.

What do you think? Is missions for us?

—*Bored Back East*

Dear Bored,

Yes, missions is for you. When Jesus told his followers it was time to go and make disciples in all nations, he was talking to all of them—and none of them were ordained clergy.

Jesus called people from all walks of life—fishermen, political activists, tax collectors. He recruited common folk as well as natural leaders, wealthy people as well as many who lived from hand to mouth, educated as well as some who seemed rather dense.

This is the motley crew to whom Jesus said, *The harvest is plentiful but the workers are few. Ask the Lord of the harvest, therefore, to send out workers into his harvest field* (Matt. 9:37-38). So it seems to me that first of all Jesus is asking you to pray about this matter of missions.

Prayers with Wheels

There's a funny thing about prayer. Rarely do I pray for more than a few minutes when I think of something I can do to help bring about the answer to my own prayer. Jesus must have noticed this same thing, because right after telling His disciples to pray, He called them together and *gave them authority to*

*drive out evil spirits and to heal every disease and
sickness* (Matt. 10:1). And then Jesus sent them out as
missionaries with a list of instructions of what to do
and how to behave (read Matthew 10).

You wouldn't understand if I told you it is
important to put *wheels* to your prayers, so I will be a
good cross cultural communicator and tell you to put
legs to your prayers. As a disciple of Jesus, you can
assume He will ask you to do the same things He
asked His other disciples to do. And He will also give
you the authority and ability to carry out your
assignment.

You are already well equipped for ministry. You
and your wife have a good education, professional
skills and work experience that can be useful most
anywhere in the world. You should notify our mission
board of your willingness to serve wherever there is
a need.

Take a Walk on Bored Walk

Now, as for your boredom, that is another
matter. You seem to be under the impression that
missionary work brings a constant thrill or emotional
high. It's true that most missionaries experience a
gratifying sense of peace, knowing they are obedient

to God. But their work is often physically exhausting, emotionally demanding, and frequently *boring.*

Whether you are building a business or building the Kingdom, work is work. The bigger the field, the greater the boredom. I can plow a small garden as if by magic in a very few minutes. But give me a 60-acre field to plow and it will take *days.* Each time around the field I am a few inches closer to being done, but you wouldn't know it based on the boredom index!

So please don't use boredom as a measure of your value or the importance of your work. Often there is no other pathway to success than doing just what you said you want to avoid—lock into a groove (I would call it a dead furrow) and stay there for 40 years, or until the job is done, or you run out of gas.

Do all work as unto the Lord, follow Him closely, and keep your heart and mind in Christ Jesus. Then you will be ready to follow Him where and when He leads. And don't be surprised, some day, if that "screaming bundle of dirty diaper" you mentioned is part of the package of your life that must be offered in humble obedience to our great God and Savior.

Discouraged, But Not About My Lawn

Dear Ferguson:

Here in Canada we get a lot of American news. It looks to me like the United States is in dramatic moral and spiritual as well as financial decline. I wish I could say things are better in Canada. Truthfully, they're not. If you watch CNN or any other world news, you see the entire globe going from bad to worse before our eyes.

Here is what I want to know. Do you ever get discouraged about the way this world is going? And if so, what do you do about it? You impress me to be an honest old tractor, so I know you won't lie to me the way a lot of the other media seems to.

—Discouraged, Eh?

Dear Eh,

You must know that for a considerable time I was the very *definition* of discouragement. Now that God has rebuilt me and is helping me operate according to shop manual specifications, I could maybe claim I no longer get discouraged. In fact, that is mainly true, but only because I have learned to *fight back*.

I battle discouragement by reading my Bible each morning. Here I see that God, the Creator and Sustainer of the universe, is indeed in control of everything—even the chaos.

You are partly right in saying, "The entire globe is going from bad to worse." However, it is only bad things that go from bad to worse. Good things go from good to better. Missionaries have a big role in the improving conditions worldwide.

If you read only the news, watch CNN, or look around you in Canada, you won't realize this, but the number of Christians is growing faster than world population growth.

I am told that about one in nine of the world's seven billion or so people are now Christians— tremendous progress in just the past 50 years. Much of this growth is in places where suffering is an expected part of the Christian walk. You can expect to suffer, too, as history moves toward the harvest.

Getting On Toward Harvest

I believe Jesus would have simply *adored* tractors had we been invented in time for Him to meet us. And *cultivators* would have been one of His favorite attachments. But, since He didn't have us as a frame of reference, He told the parable of the weeds instead. He said, *The kingdom of heaven is like a man who sowed good seed in his field. But while everyone was sleeping, his enemy came and sowed weeds among the wheat, and went away. When the wheat sprouted and formed heads, then the weeds also appeared.*

When the servants asked what to do about the weeds, the master said **not** to pull the weeds, *because while you are pulling the weeds, you may root up the wheat with them. Let both grow together until the harvest. At that time I will collect the weeds to be burned, then gather the wheat and bring it into my barn* (Matt: 24-30).

So, that is why the bad gets worse and the good gets better—we are getting on toward harvest time.

Weed 'N Feed

Nowadays we like to think we can get rid of the bad while keeping the good. We tractors often drive between rows of grain with cultivators to root out weeds. More recently, chemicals have some success with this.

One day last spring my owner plunked a paper sack of *Weed 'N Feed* down on the floor in front of me.

On the bag it said, "Weed Control With Lawn Fertilizer. Apply When Weeds Are Growing."

I read on. There was nitrogen, phosphate, and potash to make grass flourish, as well as toxic ingredients that attack such weeds as burdock, dandelion, oxalis, pigweed, poison ivy, ragweed, spurge and thistle.

Do not imagine one dose of *Weed 'N Feed* permanently cures your lawn. Frequent application is needed. But the theological implication seems obvious to me—the very troubles in life that destroy wicked people can build up righteous people. Frogs that plagued Egyptians were perhaps had for supper by followers of Moses. Or, maybe not....

But I know for a fact that fire burns away dross but purifies silver. The same wind that blows away chaff cleans good grain.

So we must not be discouraged even though weeds persist, for the Gardener has all things well in hand. The gates of hell cannot prevail against the onslaught of Great Commission people.

God Is Not Like *This* Farmer

Dear Ferguson:

My first wife divorced me because I was always gone. I was, but I was very successful in my business and have made good money now for two decades.

My second wife likes having the money so she puts up with me. And we have some pretty good times. I never did understand people who claim money can't buy happiness.

My lawyer says that in the process of succeeding at work I stepped on some folks, maybe a bit too hard, and it will take some fancy footwork for us to hold everything together.

The hot water we're in has got me asking hard questions about ethics and justice, so recently we started going to church. I think maybe I can use a little bit of my money on worthy projects like missions and was wondering what you think of my idea.

—*In Securities*

Dear Insecure,

Back in 1948 when I was fresh off the assembly line, my very first job was to drive around in a field that had been unattended for several years. Brush and weeds and grass grew high over my head.

My driver had to stand up to see where we were going. Every once in a while he would stomp on my clutch, jump down to the ground, and slash away the undergrowth. In the middle of his cutting would be a young oak tree, or a tender maple, competing for survival.

I soon began watching out for baby trees myself. However, I kept wanting to stop and single out what turned out to be a nasty old burdock. This weed with its wide leaves and green color can look suspiciously like a young oak. But instead of acorns it grows sticky cockleburs.

And what I at first thought were young maple trees often turned out to be new grape vines. I was fooled by young grape leaves that seemed much like maple leaves. Then I noticed that the grape vines had very different behavior than the maples—they wrapped clutching tentacles around neighboring growth and climbed on others to reach the sunlight.

The burdock was exposed by its fruit, the grape vine by its behavior. I was soon able to recognize desirable trees from impostors. The farmer first staked up the trees, then destroyed all surrounding growth.

Driving It Home

Why would I tell you about something that happened 45 years ago? Because I recently visited that same field. What a surprise! The burdock-looking oaklings were now towering and layered in rippling bark. Tender maples had become majestic and the birds of the air built their nests among the high branches. Looking down, I saw that any weeds had long since become mulch for the forest.

You have been missing the point all these years. What you have matters little, but *who* you are is of utmost significance. Judging from what you wrote, it is right and good that you and all your works of 20 years should be destroyed. Find a Bible and read the book called *Proverbs* to discover why this should be so.

For example, in Proverbs 15:6 you will read, *The house of the righteous contains great treasure, but the income of the wicked brings them trouble.*

I do have one piece of good news for you. The farmer in my experience did not have the power to transform a burdock into an oak, or a grape vine into a maple. However, God does have the ability to clean your evil and greedy heart and make you into a new man. But first you must turn to him the way Zacchaeus did. Please read Luke 19:1-10 to see what I mean.

You asked what I thought of the idea of using a little bit of your money for missions. I think that is a dreadful idea. It will make you an even more conceited and self-righteous fool. Not until you have learned to do justice, to love kindness, and to walk humbly with your God will your money be of much redemptive use for anyone at all.

A Church-Planting Recipe

Dear Ferguson:

As I tucked in my garden for the winter I wondered about the connections between planting gardens and planting churches. With your background in both missions and farming, I wonder if you have some thoughts on that.

—Wintering in Nebraska

Dear WIN,

Let me tell you about Carmena Capp. She is from Alaska, so she knows all about winter, but she was a missionary in South Africa, so she also knows all about church planting. Best of all, Carmena is a landscape designer. More than one Bible seminary campus has blossomed under her thumb. I thought that if Carmena could grow a college campus, surely she would know how to grow a church. I asked her about this, and here is what I learned:

1. Find a bare spot (a community without a Christian witness), dig a deep, square hole (pick any old spot for holding meetings).

2. Fill the hole two-thirds full with a mixture of peat, pot ash, lime, compost, and topsoil (readily available in any community).

3. Transplant several healthy shoots from an existing branch of the church.

4. Surround the planting with a deep layer of grass clippings, wood chips, and other mulch. The mulch is to protect roots from sun. It also retains moisture and keeps down weeds, conserving the energy and resources of the soil. Congregations need to make that kind of blanket around every new convert and child.

5. Water well. Every plant needs water in order to absorb food. But be careful not to surface water only, or the roots will come up to reach the water, and then die in the next drought. To plant a church properly you must water deeply. Jesus said that he was the water of life. We must preach and live Jesus to those we try to reach.

Carmena told me, "One of the most beautiful experiences of my many years in Africa was to drive through a desperately dry, brown desert, then to crest a hill and see a deep green 'snake' of trees in a valley below. The stream bed they followed was dry,

but very deep roots caused these trees to flourish."
People grounded in Jesus will survive.

6.   Feed routinely with heavy doses of solid Bible
      teaching. Feeding is very important. Unless you
      feed, you might as well not plant.

"To plant something and then not care for it is a sin
against creation—it is to bring life into being, and
then let it die." Carmena adds, "Do you know why
sloth is one of the Seven Deadly Sins? I never
understood why until one day working in my garden.
It is because the beauty and the order which God
intended never comes to be unless you care for it as
Adam was assigned in the garden." As you feed, pray
that the life-giving rain of the Holy Spirit's presence
will, along with the sunshine of God's love and mercy,
make an ideal growth climate.

7.   Every few years, prune back heavily, using new
      shoots to plant yet other churches. You must cut
      away that which takes too much strength from
      the plant.

Lay into the incredible fattening of ourselves—
growing our own fat trunks so much that we have no
time for outreach. The overshadowing of big
branches can crowd out the place of little branches,
taking away all the sun and nutrients.

Carmena's advice is to "prune back the old enough that the young can find a place in the sun. If your garden is a power struggle for each plant to find a place in the sun, you don't have a garden, you have a jungle! The purpose of a garden is for each plant to glorify God. Just so, each Christian should have a place and function and be allowed to develop into something truly beautiful that can glorify the Creator."

Now we must review step 3, *transplanting.* Better to transplant when the tree is young—not so very young that it can't survive alone, but don't wait until its roots are too deep—for then you can't get them all out.

Many Christians are so very deeply planted in their own culture and need for luxury, they simply can't adjust in a way that makes it possible for them to communicate the gospel to other cultures. Materialistic, entertainment oriented Christians have difficulty communicating the gospel, not because of a lack of means but because of their crippling dependency on things. The missionary enterprise today needs more people willing to be transplants.

The Yoke's On Me

Dear Ferguson:

I understand you have traveled to southern Africa. What a remarkable thing for a tractor to visit a mission field! I am very curious about the journey you took, and what you learned, if anything.

—Just Wondering

Dear Wonder,

What a dreadful thing it is for an old tractor like me to go on a journey half way around the world! I thought being trucked to Mexico for my missionary career was quite a thrilling and sensible thing—but riding on a *boat* to Africa—my, my! International travel can be such a fuss—what a complicated business—unless you enjoy that sort of thing.

What did I learn? I learned to be thankful. And I learned to pray with far greater insight than ever before.

It was a special treat to meet my distant South African relative, M. Ferguson. She is much younger than I and ever so much better looking. More importantly, she has more power than I do, and as a national leader, she has a profound understanding of the culture and language over there.

What a heritage, for she parks in the very garage where the likes of J. W. Haley and James Rice would have lived and worked. All this gives M. Ferguson greater ability than I could ever have as she gracefully and efficiently ministers in South Africa.

I confess that until now I had a certain mistrust of national leaders. I felt more comfortable in providing financial and prayer support to missionaries from my homeland who I knew personally to be reliable, hard workers. I wasn't sure if unknown South Africans had the same abilities.

I also confess to feeling guilty about spending all the money it took to make this visit. Shouldn't I simply have given that money? Perhaps. Yet I felt compelled to find out for myself more of the way God works.

And what a reassuring experience it was. The Lord showed me that if I hadn't spent the money on travel, I would more likely have frittered it away in some useless way rather than giving it to missions.

It turns out that my travel expenses were more of a down payment—just the beginning of a renewed commitment to missions. As a result of my trip I will pray more intelligently and give more generously of all my future time and income.

Although we are not oxen, M. Ferguson and I have become yoke fellows. I know the mental image of two tractors yoked together is a startling one, but in the Kingdom of Heaven, all things are possible.

A Cheeky Proposition

Dear Ferguson:

I often wonder whether God really has a plan for my life, or do preachers just say that to boost my ego? What difference does it make whether I devote my life to God or just live for myself?

—Making Plans

Dear Plans,

I once had a chipmunk neighbor I called Cheeks, because that was her dominant feature. I seldom saw her actually eat an acorn. Usually she just tucked them into her cheeks for transport.

Cheeks was cute and loveable, but not bright. She had much greater capacity in her cheeks than in her brain. She could bury a dozen acorns for every one she could locate later. Does this mean her much scurrying about was to no purpose? Of course not. Cheeky though she may have been, she was (without knowing it) a planter of oak trees.

God made Cheeks that way—highly motivated to provide for her own needs. And she packed away enough for many others as well. But Cheeks knew nothing of God's plan. She thought she was just doing a good job of surviving the winter.

It may be that some humans manage to live an entirely selfish life, just like Cheeks, and still make a meaningful contribution to the Kingdom of God, but I don't recommend it.

You see, unlike Cheeks, you are made in God's image. God has much larger plans for you than He has for any cheeky little rodent. Best of all, unlike Cheeks, you can *understand* that plan and enjoy watching it unfold.

God wants to give you an eternal life of fellowship with Himself. This is a very great reward that you will forfeit if you live for yourself rather than giving your life to Him. Right now, you must humble yourself before God. Ask Him to forgive you for all the pride and selfishness you are feeling.

Now, to answer your question, I believe absolutely that God has a special plan for your life, but I don't know what that plan is. God is the one who knows. Ask *Him!* He won't write you a letter, of course, but He will unfold that plan. And when He does, you must obey and do what He asks you to do. Only in obedience will you discover His plan and realize it is far better than your own.

No-Till Theology

Dear Ferguson:

No doubt you are aware of the modern no-till farming method in which we harvest last year's crop, then drill this year's seed next to the old rows without plowing. This saves both time and fuel. Spraying keeps the weeds down, and a good crop can be expected.

Are you aware of any similar ways to make missions more efficient and cost-effective while producing the same harvest?

—Professor Green Thumb, MSU

Dear Thumb,

I admire all efforts to save time and money. Even more, I admire efforts to bring in a harvest of people needing God. But I notice that some hi-tech, low effort methods produce *less* yield at much *greater* expense.

For example, in many places labor is cheap and chemical fertilizers and weed controllers expensive. Big machinery needed for spraying chemicals and drilling seed are too expensive and impossible to use on small plots on steep hills—there are many complications.

In the same way, more than a few cleverly-hatched campaigns and wagon-loads of church programs keep lots of well-meaning people very busy, but keep your eye on the fruit they produce. In some cases you are bound to be very disappointed.

Meanwhile on the mission front, we often see outstanding results in developing countries under the low profile, high individual effort of poor people with nothing but time. When they use their time to build relationships and disciple new believers, dramatic progress is usually possible.

To understand this you must imagine a field where the few seeds the farmer plants and cultivates soon take up the farming business themselves—planting and cultivating still others until the entire field is fully planted and carefully tended.

No-till farming may work in some instances, but no-till relationships and no-till theology are for the birds.

A Plot Thickens

Dear Ferguson:

Are you real or imaginary? Sometimes I think you are human, but you claim to be a tractor—and tractors can't talk!

—*I'm Confused*

Dear Confused,

Your question implies that if something is imaginary, then it can't be real. I disagree. I think imagination is *something,* and that makes it *real.*

True, I am fictitious, but great fiction is about *reality.* You could say that I am every bit as real as *The Velveteen Rabbit.*

As to whether I represent great fiction, you will be interested to know that the magazine editor sent an entire year of my columns to the Evangelical Press Association (EPA) for evaluation under the "fiction" category. Here is what the EPA judge said about me:

No question that Ferguson is easy to like, easy to read, and offers clever and cogent advice—but strictly speaking she just isn't a work of fiction (no plot, for instance). However, Ferguson does what she's intended to do, much better than Dear Abby.

The judge gave me a score of seven out of a possible ten for being believable and credible, and said my writing is "satisfactory." Not having read my actual tractor-biography, the judge did not know either about the plot of my personal story or the plot where I was planted.

My conviction is that to "grow where you're planted" makes for the best imaginable plot. Do that, and you will become just as real as I am.

Dear Ferguson:

Are you married? If so, do you have any children or grandchildren? As a grandmother myself, I wonder if there is anything I can do to influence my loved ones to be more interested in missions. I thought perhaps you might have some ideas along these lines.

—*Grandma Toolie*

Dear Grandma,

Pedro Moura is a farmer in Brazil. He has given all of his ten children their own plot of ground to cultivate. Vegetation on each well-tended plot thickens, which benefits everyone concerned. Hold that thought in mind while I answer your first question....

Just as it is in heaven among angels, so it is on earth among tractors—there is no giving or taking in marriage. Hence, I have never been married, and I must also admit to the biological fact that tractors rarely have children (no known cases so far).

While many of us came from the same mold, you couldn't call us clones, for we tend toward mutation. I myself started out with a six-volt electrical system, but at my conversion was transformed to 12-volt, from my battery right down to my alternator. In addition, my newish tires are larger than factory specifications, and I believe I have had four or five radiator transplants.

That tractors do not have children is why Amish farmers prefer horses. True, when horses break down you shoot them, but they replace themselves with offspring. Tractors are over-rated. We require money for maintenance, fuel, and repairs. We are dangerous on hills and rocky terrain, and we never remember the way home.

By contrast, a well-trained beast is often more economical and effective. The long-eared burro needs a boy only to fill his large rubber saddle-bag flasks at the watering hole. The water flasks full, the load heavy, the sun hot, the burro trudging home is a daily sight. And a little child can lead him.

Ah, children! Grandchildren! For myself, I have only the mice that nest in my toolbox and attend class meeting. I heard that John Wesley recommended this, so I immediately started one. I hold my mice accountable for their moral and spiritual conduct, and I teach them a Bible lesson each week.

You should do the same for each of your grandchildren—in person if they are close by, or write to them if they are far away, and call or Skype once in a while to touch base. Also, pray for them daily.

Be like Pedro Moura—*Plot* for the future of your children. They will prosper for it, and surely the Great Commission will not be hindered.

A Quackgrass Church

Dear Ferguson:

I am new to church and there is a lot that I don't understand. Example: Last Sunday a visiting bishop said we are a connectional church. What does that mean, and does it have anything to do with missions?

—*Newly Connected*

Dear Connected,

Connectional means we are all hooked together, like quackgrass with an underground root system. Kill us off in one section of the lawn and we pop up elsewhere. It means help may arrive from Florida for earthquake victims in California. Chase us out of Kenya and we'll turn up stronger than ever in Burundi. Plant a church in Costa Rica and soon connected Christians will crop up in Columbia.

The bishop who spoke in your church tells me this: "Even months in a compost pit will not break down quackgrass!"

Quackgrass is a *perennial* plant, which pretty much means it will live forever. Now *that's* the kind of Jesus follower to be!

Dear Ferguson:

I asked an older lady in my church if our missions group "prays through the 10/40 window."

She squinted at me and said, "Now we see through a glass, darkly, but then face to face."

Ding dong! I don't know what she was talking about, and she probably thought the "10/40 window" was a term used by truckers, as in "Ten-forty, good buddy, I got you in my window...."

Finally, I convinced her it was a mission question I was wondering about.

"Oh!" she said. "If you have a question about missions, ask Ferguson!" So here I am!

—Good Buddy in New Jersey

Dear Jersey,

Of course, your reference to the "10/40 window" has to do with the parallel lines on the globe.

Missions researchers have noticed that the vast majority of people yet unreached with the gospel live between the 10th parallel south and the 40th parallel north of the equator. This swatch of our planet takes in much of Africa as well as of such Asian countries as India, Nepal, Laos, and China.

This portion of the globe encompasses almost the entire Arab world where the Muslim faith dominates.

As you know, to "pray through the 10/40 window" means to join the many thousands of Christians who are urgently talking with God about the prospects of breaking through powerful spiritual barriers and flooding this part of the world with the Good News about Jesus. They are also praying that many thousands of new missionaries will be mobilized to reach into these areas with the gospel.

Researchers think there are around 11,000 people groups in the world (as distinguished by language). Probably about 3,000 such groups still do not have any form of Christian witness among them and are "unreached."

As you pray, please remember that it is *people* who reach other people, and a "people group" is not "reached" until a viable church has been planted in the culture. This requires more than just showing a film, passing out some tracts, or even translating the Bible into that language.

And that is why, even though they are often criticized, missionaries who plant churches of a particular denomination play a very important role.

114

Baby Christians in any culture need someone who will nurture and guide them. They need a church. They need the fellowship of like-minded believers. They need to be connected. Otherwise they will quickly fall back into old beliefs and behaviors. The goal of both missions work and church planting is to be finders *and* keepers.

Brick & Mortar vs. Hearts of Flesh

Dear Ferguson:

We're having a building campaign at my church. They want to move us out near the highway where we can have greater visibility and a bigger sanctuary so we don't have to hold multiple services.

I keep thinking, what an astonishing sum of money to spend on cement and steel. I wonder what God's priorities might be if we would give an equal amount of cash to something that really mattered.

If the new building is so important, why do I feel confused? Am I wrong to oppose this move? And what should I do with my gifts?

My heart just isn't in this. I would rather invest in missions or direct ministry to the needs of people, but the pressure is on to put money in the building fund. Any insights you may have will be thoughtfully considered.

—Mortar-ly Ill

Dear Ill,

A thick and lush wisteria vine grew over an arbor against the south side of a farm house where I lived. Magnificent and graceful, the wisteria shaded

116

the house from summer heat. Children played under this cool shelter.

After 30 years the arbor rotted, threatening to collapse and bring the wisteria down with it.

To save the wisteria, the farmer carefully took apart and rebuilt the trellised arbor, one piece at a time. The wisteria was also pruned and dead wood trimmed out.

"Ouch! Help! No!" yelled the wisteria. "You're *killing* me!"

"Fact is," replied the farmer, "I'm *saving* you. It's just the trellis that must go. I will pour cement footings and raise a cedar framework to last another generation. In any case, your stump is now so thick and strong, you scarcely need support."

The vine was not convinced. She had lived long with one structure and could no longer distinguish the plant from the post.

The North American church is like that vine, unable to separate the church from its old framework.

Jesus himself faced this situation. Jews fondly remembered the splendid cedar and gold-plated temple of Solomon. This was destroyed, and a less noble but still impressive structure was built under the leadership of Ezra.

Even as they rebuilt the temple, an important prophecy came through Haggai: *In a little while I will once more shake the heavens and the earth. I will shake all nations, and the desired of all nations will come, and I will fill my house with glory. The glory of this house will be greater than the glory of the former house...* (Haggai 2:6-9).

Haggai was predicting a new kind of temple—as Jesus explained to the Samaritan woman in John 4:21-23: *The time has now come when you will worship the Father neither on this mountain nor in Jerusalem. True worshipers will worship the Father in spirit and truth, for they are the kind of worshipers the Father seeks.*

The temple God wants now is not a building of stones and cedar but the body of Christ, the bride of Christ, the church. Many hulking church buildings in post-Christian nations stand empty while in places as far-flung as Egypt and China the church is burgeoning all out of proportion to its real estate—scarcely a building to its name.

Indeed, a structure could hardly be built to house the prayer meetings that took place in Korea in the late 20th century when 700,000 people met in one place at one time.

Now to your questions. If you feel confused, perhaps it is because the message of Jesus does not square with the message from your church building committee. If so, stick with the message of Jesus.

As to whether you are wrong to oppose the move, perhaps you are. Jesus didn't oppose the temple building so much as he realized it to be obsolete. Thanks to the sacrifice of His own life, the temple has become as irrelevant as the sacrifices performed there.

On this issue the temple authorities found grounds for crucifying Jesus. Since you share His vision, you will also likely share in His suffering.

The people who want buildings are blind to the beauty of the new temple and will not understand your vision. Let them give to what pleases them. As for you, give to what pleases God.

So honor Him by making your gift to God Himself. Lay your gift at the feet of the apostles—no strings attached—as Barnabas did in Acts 4:37. In so doing you will be blessed, for God promises to honor those who honor Him.

Seeing Through the Steel Wool

Dear Ferguson:

That last column of yours made me real mad. You basically said church buildings are obsolete. I don't generally write to people like you, but after reading that page I fired up my computer and started in. *I'll have your hide,* I thought. Then I remembered you're just an old tractor with thick metal skin.

Still, what I wrote wasn't nice. It also wasn't true, I realized after thinking on it all day while stringing some rafters. So last night I deleted what I wrote, and before starting over I reread your column.

On the second read, what jumped out at me was *Mortar-ly Ill's* statement, "What an astonishing sum of money to spend on cement and steel."

I got to wondering about priorities and balance. You see, I am a builder by trade—a general contractor. I have built several churches. I can tell you the price of just about anything at the lumberyard, as well as how much it costs per hour for professional workers.

It *is* a ton of money. It got me to thinking: *Maybe I have been focusing on building real estate instead of building the church!* How can I keep my priorities straight? Any ideas?

—Generally Contracting

Dear General,

I am not surprised you were angry, and you're really kind of small potatoes as a builder compared to some of those old timers. To build his temple, Solomon recruited 30,000 laborers from all over Israel, plus an additional 70,000 workers on regular payroll, 80,000 stonecutters and 3,300 foremen (1 Kings 5-8).

Herod's temple at the time of Christ was not so elaborate. Yet, when Jesus claimed something greater than the temple had arrived, you can see how such a statement could make the Jews angry.

Buildings are often easy to pay for compared with really working in building the Kingdom. Buildings can keep people busy, thinking they are doing something important for God, when what God actually wants is for us to build *His temple*—the one that will stand up to the gates of hell.

The devil has tried to pull the steel wool over our eyes. He doesn't want us to see the main task of the church, which is to tell everyone about Jesus, and then to disciple them in the faith.

This is best done, not with buildings, but with relationships. As Aleksandr Solzhenitsyn told many Russian peasants during his train trip across that nation, "Religion is passed from man to man as an intimate gift."

Sharing the good news has wrapped up in it the salvation of others, as well as our own salvation. In Romans 10:9-10 the Apostle Paul reduced the gospel to its essence when he wrote, *If you confess with your mouth, "Jesus is Lord," and believe in your heart that God raised him from the dead, you will be saved. For it is with your heart that you believe and are justified, and it is with your mouth that you confess and are saved.*

Most of us seldom confess with our mouths, nor do we routinely introduce others to the One whom we claim is our best friend. But those who do are building the real church.

This is not to say buildings are bad. They are often necessary and useful, and some building programs are long overdue. But when such programs are accompanied by excessive debt and become the main priority of a church, they do carry with them a grave danger.

If you can both build a facility and build the true kingdom (as is frequently the case), then you have struck an important balance. I would heartily endorse a construction campaign in which church members shared their faith with an unbeliever once for every $1,000 raised.

However, it is easy to see our own needs while ignoring the needs of others. If we are to become world mission people, we must take seriously the words of the One who said, "Unless you deny yourself, take up your cross, and follow Me, you cannot be My disciple."

When those who stay home practice a level of obedience equal to that of those who go, the true temple will be full of the glory of God, both at home and around the globe.

One Astonished Missionary

Dear Ferguson:

I am trying to make a decision about whether to go to college, and if so, what college to attend. It's hard to decide because it all depends on what I want to do with my life! If you can answer my basic question, that will help. I am wondering, *what is the most important work a Christian can do?*

—*Weighing My Options*

Dear Weighing,

It has been taught for many centuries that the basic purpose of our existence is to love God and enjoy Him forever. How we do that is an individual thing, hinging on the sovereign will of God, the gifts He gives us, and the extent to which we obey Him.

Consider my own life. I could never swing steel beams into place on a 60-story building because I am not a crane. Rather, I have natural endowments in the direction of grooming the soil and taking care of plants that have been carefully organized into rows in a field.

I can also pull heavy objects across rugged terrain, mow grass, and do various other down-to-earth functions. A farm is a wonderful place for me because I was created just for this particular type of service.

So you must first ask yourself: *What is the particular work for which God has uniquely suited me?* If you can decide this, you will have made good progress in deciding which of your natural abilities and interests to cultivate.

One line of work is not more important than another line of work, but you would do well to look down the line to see the consequences of your work. Does it help people or hurt people. If it helps people in some way, then surely God approves.

You see, *people* are what matter most. Serving people is the most valuable use of our time. So I urge you to look for ways to become a servant. And as you look, you will also do well to remember that God is full of surprises. I am utterly astonished to have been a missionary! Of all possible jobs, this one was never prominently displayed on the Ferguson advertising literature (but I may not have seen all the fine print).

Which just goes to show, what you are now is just a shadow of what you can become if you walk faithfully in complete obedience to the leading of the Holy Spirit. In *My Utmost for His Highness*, Oswald

Chambers said, "Beware of harking back to what you were once when God wants you to be something you have never been."

What are we so far? We are the Lord's humble servants, a growing army of kingdom people, doing whatever it takes to live for Jesus and build His church.

What are we ultimately to become? The Apostle John shows us: *Dear Friends, now we are children of God, and we know that when [Jesus] appears we shall be like Him, for we shall see Him as He is* (1John 3:2).

So my advice is this: No matter what else you do in this life, see that you do all you can to become like Jesus. If college can help you achieve this calling, then by all means go!

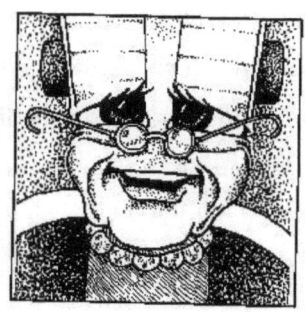

www.ingramcontent.com/pod-product-compliance
Lightning Source LLC
Chambersburg PA
CBHW031835170626
46807CB00004B/1470